DISTRESS FLAG

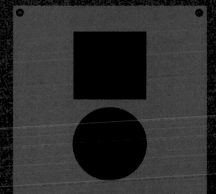

PARACHUTE FLARE

S O S
... --- ...

DISTRESS SIGNAL

BILLY PUGH BASKET

COMPASS

For Tien and Reid

RESCUE

E
AUS
c.1
2/17
$20.00
Forever Books

RESCUE SQUAD No. 9

by Mike Austin

Random House 🏠 New York

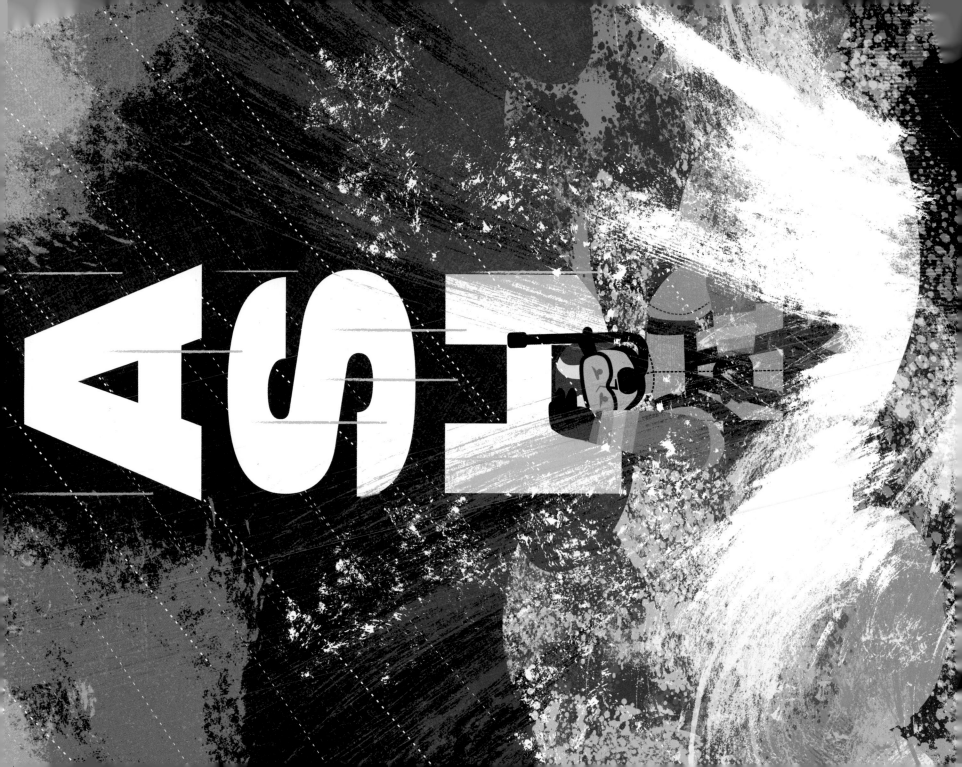

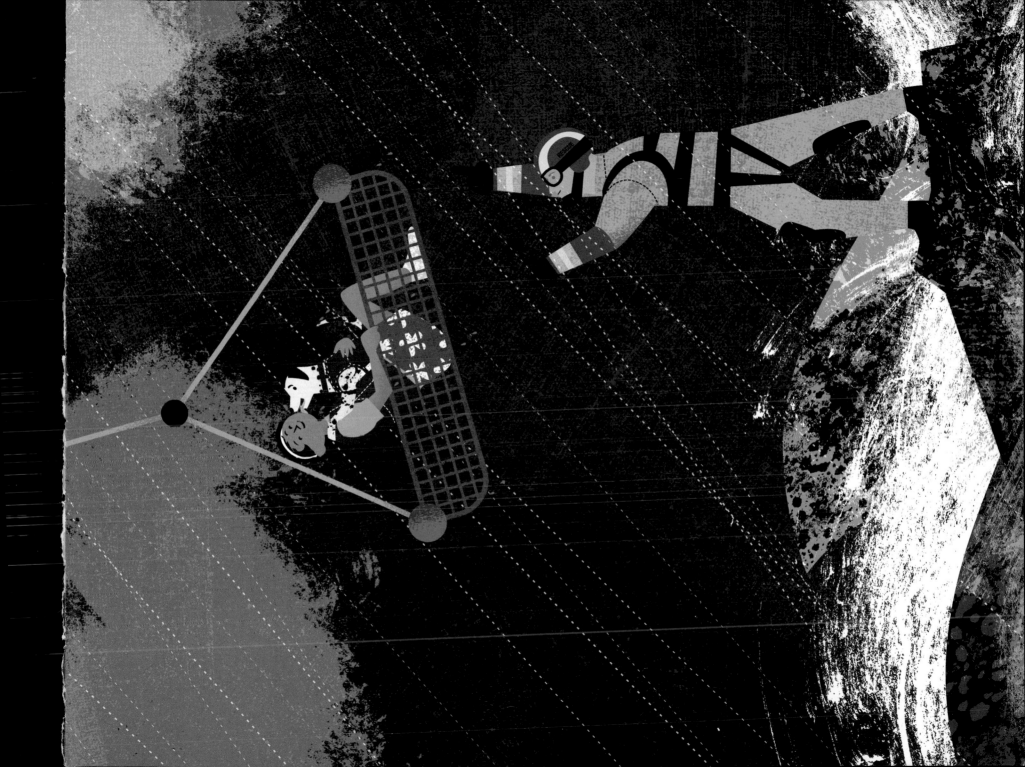

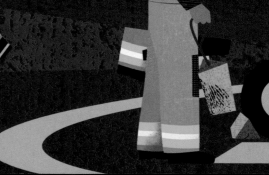

RESCUE **9**

SUPPLIES

SUPPLIES SUPPLIES SUPPLIES

Hooray! Hooray!

ANNUAL REGATTA!

RESCUE 9

Thank you, Rescue Squad No. 9!

RESCUE 9

SEA RACER

Do Your Part—Be Water Smart*

- Make sure everyone in your family learns to swim well. Enroll in age-appropriate Red Cross water orientation and learn-to-swim courses.

- Swim in areas supervised by lifeguards.

- Always swim with a buddy; never swim alone. Even at a public pool or a lifeguarded beach, use the buddy system.

- Never leave a child unattended near water, and do not trust a child's life to another child. Teach children to always ask permission to go near water.

- Have children or inexperienced swimmers wear U.S. Coast Guard–approved life jackets around water, but do not rely on life jackets alone.

- Establish water safety rules for your family, and be sure they are always followed. For example, do not let anyone play around drains and suction fittings, do not allow swimmers to hyperventilate (take more than one deep breath) before playing or swimming underwater, and do not let them have breath-holding contests.

- Even if you do not plan on swimming, be cautious around natural bodies of water, including the ocean, rivers, and lakes. Cold temperatures, currents, and underwater hazards can make a fall into these bodies of water dangerous.

- If you go boating, wear a U.S. Coast Guard–approved life jacket!

- Learn how to respond to a water emergency, including how to perform CPR.

* Water safety tips provided by the American Red Cross, redcross.org/watersafetytips. To find classes about learning to swim, water safety, and CPR, visit redcross.org/takeaclass.

FLASHLIGHT

LIFE VEST

AIR HORN

RESCUE
9

HELMET

RING BUOY